HOPSCOTCH FAIRY TALES

D0301298

Cinderella

by Anne Cassidy and Jan McCafferty

W

FRANKLIN WATTS

LONDON • SYDNEY

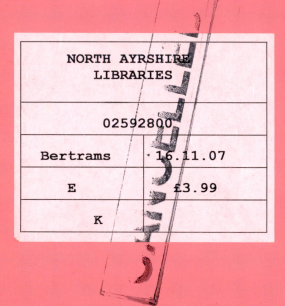

Once upon a time there was
a girl called Cinderella.
She was not happy.

Cinderella had two stepsisters.
One was tall and one was small.
They made Cinderella work all
day long.

The stepsisters made Cinderella
wear horrible clothes.

And they made her sleep
by the fireplace.

One day a letter arrived.

"It's from the prince!" said the tall stepsister. "There's a ball at the palace!" said the small stepsister.

Everyone was excited – even Cinderella. The stepsisters told her: "But *you* can't come!"

After the stepsisters left for
the ball, Cinderella sat
by the fireplace.

"It's not fair," she said.

"I'd love to go to the ball!"

Suddenly there was a big flash.

It was a fairy with a wand!

"I'm your fairy godmother," she said.
"Now you can go to the ball!"

The fairy godmother waved her
wand. In another flash, Cinderella
had a new dress and sparkling
glass slippers.

Then the fairy godmother
saw a pumpkin ...

four black mice ...

and a rat.

She waved her wand and, in a
flash, there were four black horses
and a handsome coach driver.
"Here is your coach," she said.

"Now I really can go to the ball!"
said Cinderella.

"Be back before the clock strikes
twelve!" said the fairy godmother.

"Bye bye!" Cinderella said.
"Don't forget to be back by
twelve!" the fairy godmother
shouted.

When Cinderella arrived at the
ball, everyone looked at her.
"Who is she?" they wondered.

The stepsisters stared, and the
prince couldn't take his eyes off her.

"Will you dance with me?"
the prince asked Cinderella.

The prince and Cinderella
danced ...

and danced …

and danced all night.

Suddenly Cinderella heard the clock strike twelve. She ran out of the palace. The prince ran after her, but Cinderella was gone.

"Look! She has left a glass slipper behind!" the prince cried.

"Whoever can fit into the slipper will be my princess," he promised.

The prince searched every house in the land. Finally, he arrived at Cinderella's house.

First, the tall sister tried the slipper on. But it was much too small.

Then the small stepsister tried it on. But it was much too big.

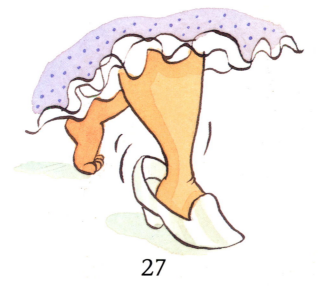

"Now this girl must try it on!"
the prince said.

"But that's just Cinderella!"
laughed the stepsisters.

Cinderella sat down. She tried the glass slipper on. It fitted perfectly.

"Will you be my princess?" asked
the prince. Cinderella agreed and
they lived happily ever after.

31

Hopscotch has been specially designed to fit the requirements of the National Literacy Strategy. It offers real books by top authors and illustrators for children developing their reading skills. There are 43 Hopscotch stories to choose from:

Marvin, the Blue Pig
ISBN 978 0 7496 4619 6

Plip and Plop
ISBN 978 0 7496 4620 2

The Queen's Dragon
ISBN 978 0 7496 4618 9

Flora McQuack
ISBN 978 0 7496 4621 9

Willie the Whale
ISBN 978 0 7496 4623 3

Naughty Nancy
ISBN 978 0 7496 4622 6

Run!
ISBN 978 0 7496 4705 6

The Playground Snake
ISBN 978 0 7496 4706 3

"Sausages!"
ISBN 978 0 7496 4707 0

The Truth about Hansel and Gretel
ISBN 978 0 7496 4708 7

Pippin's Big Jump
ISBN 978 0 7496 4710 0

Whose Birthday Is It?
ISBN 978 0 7496 4709 4

The Princess and the Frog
ISBN 978 0 7496 5129 9

Flynn Flies High
ISBN 978 0 7496 5130 5

Clever Cat
ISBN 978 0 7496 5131 2

Moo!
ISBN 978 0 7496 5332 3

Izzie's Idea
ISBN 978 0 7496 5334 7

Roly-poly Rice Ball
ISBN 978 0 7496 5333 0

I Can't Stand It!
ISBN 978 0 7496 5765 9

Cockerel's Big Egg
ISBN 978 0 7496 5767 3

How to Teach a Dragon Manners
ISBN 978 0 7496 5873 1

The Truth about those Billy Goats
ISBN 978 0 7496 5766 6

Marlowe's Mum and the Tree House
ISBN 978 0 7496 5874 8

Bear in Town
ISBN 978 0 7496 5875 5

The Best Den Ever
ISBN 978 0 7496 5876 2

ADVENTURE STORIES

Aladdin and the Lamp
ISBN 978 0 7496 6678 1 *
ISBN 978 0 7496 6692 7

Blackbeard the Pirate
ISBN 978 0 7496 6676 7 *
ISBN 978 0 7496 6690 3

George and the Dragon
ISBN 978 0 7496 6677 4 *
ISBN 978 0 7496 6691 0

Jack the Giant-Killer
ISBN 978 0 7496 6680 4 *
ISBN 978 0 7496 6693 4

TALES OF KING ARTHUR

1. The Sword in the Stone
ISBN 978 0 7496 6681 1 *
ISBN 978 0 7496 6694 1

2. Arthur the King
ISBN 978 0 7496 6683 5 *
ISBN 978 0 7496 6695 8

3. The Round Table
ISBN 978 0 7496 6684 2 *
ISBN 978 0 7496 6697 2

4. Sir Lancelot and the Ice Castle
ISBN 978 0 7496 6685 9 *
ISBN 978 0 7496 6698 9

TALES OF ROBIN HOOD

Robin and the Knight
ISBN 978 0 7496 6686 6 *
ISBN 978 0 7496 6699 6

Robin and the Monk
ISBN 978 0 7496 6687 3 *
ISBN 978 0 7496 6700 9

Robin and the Friar
ISBN 978 0 7496 6688 0 *
ISBN 978 0 7496 6702 3

Robin and the Silver Arrow
ISBN 978 0 7496 6689 7 *
ISBN 978 0 7496 6703 0

FAIRY TALES

The Emperor's New Clothes
ISBN 978 0 7496 7077 1 *
ISBN 978 0 7496 7421 2

Cinderella
ISBN 978 0 7496 7073 3 *
ISBN 978 0 7496 7417 5

Snow White
ISBN 978 0 7496 7074 0 *
ISBN 978 0 7496 7418 2

Jack and the Beanstalk
ISBN 978 0 7496 7078 8 *
ISBN 978 0 7496 7422 9

The Three Billy Goats Gruff
ISBN 978 0 7496 7076 4 *
ISBN 978 0 7496 7420 5

The Pied Piper of Hamelin
ISBN 978 0 7496 7075 7 *
ISBN 978 0 7496 7419 9

* hardback